DISNEY PRINCESS

A Dream Comes True

PaRragon

Bath • New York • Cologne • Melbourne • Delhi
Hong Kong • Shenzhen • Singapore

Prince Charming had found the woman he loved. Next, he did what all men in love do, he asked, "Will you marry me?" and waited for the answer.

Cinderella said yes!

The King was thrilled to hear the news. In the hall, he gestured to a portrait of a beautiful woman. "This was my wife on our wedding day. And Cinderella shall wear the same thing. It is royal family tradition," said the King. "There is nothing more important than family traditions!"

Cinderella quietly looked at the Queen's portrait. She did not want to disappoint the King.

But following this family tradition was not easy with so many royal helpers.

Luckily, the Grand Duke had a plan.

"Here is all you need to know about royal traditions," said the Grand Duke, as he brought Cinderella a stack of books.

Cinderella read and read, trying to remember everything until, at last, she fell asleep.

In a dream, Cinderella's mother gave her a special gift. "Cinderella my love, this necklace will remind you that whenever you have a problem, if you listen to your heart, it will lead you to the answer."

Cinderella woke up.
The dream of her mother filled
her with warmth and brought a
smile to her face.

She began to search through
some of her old trunks.

With the help of the fairy
godmother, the mice and a
little magic, Cinderella found
what she was looking for –
a portrait of her mother on her
wedding day.

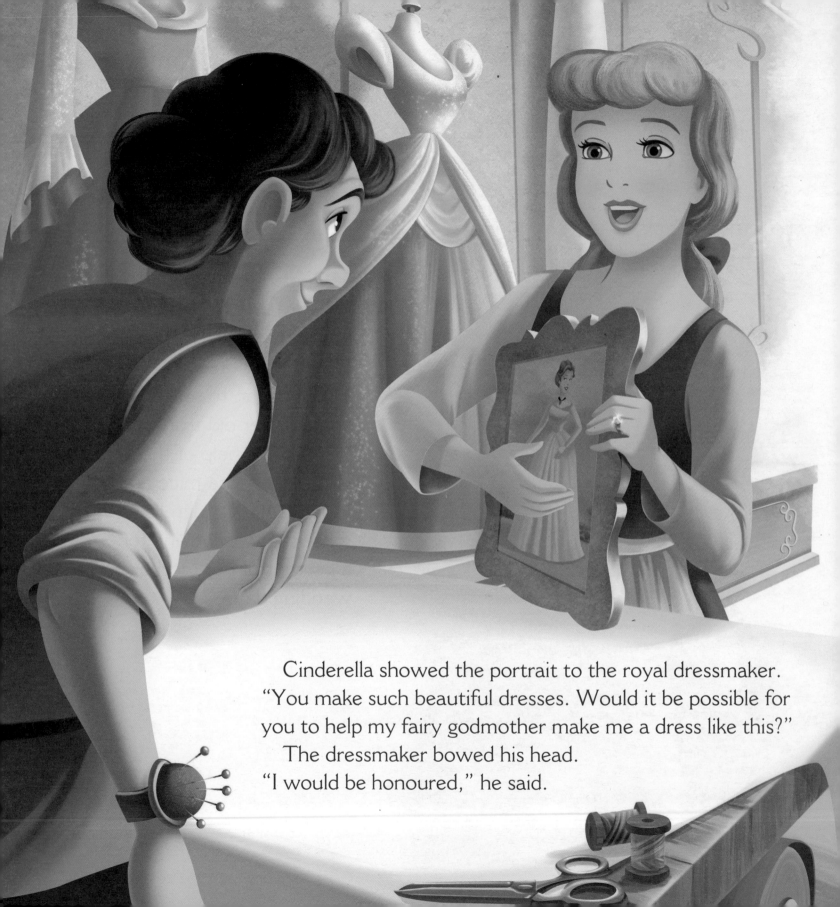

Cinderella showed the portrait to the royal dressmaker. "You make such beautiful dresses. Would it be possible for you to help my fairy godmother make me a dress like this?"

The dressmaker bowed his head.

"I would be honoured," he said.

Next, Cinderella visited the royal jeweller. "You are an artist. Do you think it would be possible to work with my mice friends and combine two necklaces into one?"

"For you I shall create the finest necklace in the kingdom," said the jeweller.

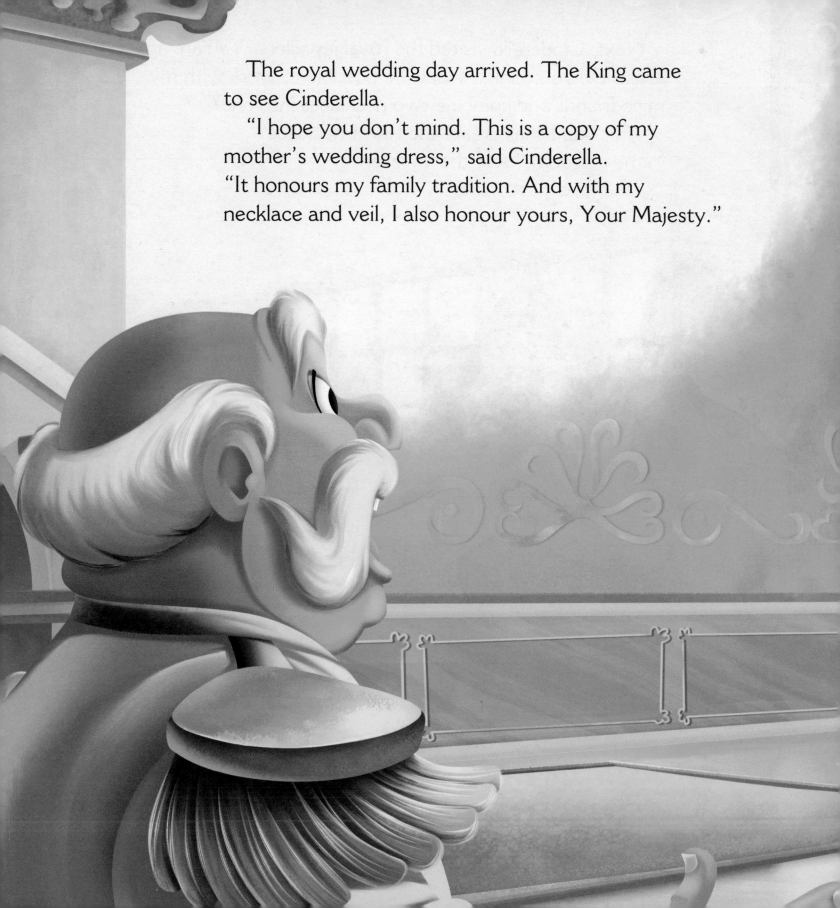

The royal wedding day arrived. The King came to see Cinderella.

"I hope you don't mind. This is a copy of my mother's wedding dress," said Cinderella. "It honours my family tradition. And with my necklace and veil, I also honour yours, Your Majesty."

The King saw that his Queen's pearls had been used to make the wedding necklace and veil. "Oh my dear girl, this is a great honour. You have blended the treasures of two families – and created a new tradition for our family."

The King proudly
offered Cinderella his arm.
"Let's not keep the
Prince waiting."

A happy King led
Cinderella down the
aisle. The guests were
thrilled. The Prince
was entranced. Even
the Grand Duke wiped
a tear from his eye.

The Prince and
Cinderella answered the
question that all brides
and grooms must answer.
"They do! They do!"
shouted Gus-Gus.

The wedding banquet was royal in every detail.

The wedding cake was a work of art.

The bouquet was beautiful!

And so, by following tradition – and her heart
– Cinderella had the wedding of her dreams!